The Greatest Inventor of All Time . . . Flint Lockwood!

adapted by Tina Gallo
illustrated by Aaron Spurgeon

SIMON SPOTLIGHT

An imprint of Simon & Schuster Children's Publishing Division
New York London Toronto Sydney New Delhi
1230 Avenue of the Americas, New York, New York 10020

For information about special discounts for bulk purchases, please contact
Simon & Schuster Special Sales at 1-866-506-1949 or business@simonandschuster.com.
Manufactured in the United States of America 0713 PH1
First Edition
2 4 6 8 10 9 7 5 3 1
ISBN 978-1-4424-9648-4
ISBN 978-1-4424-9649-1 (eBook)

Read the original book by
Judi Barrett and Ron Barrett.

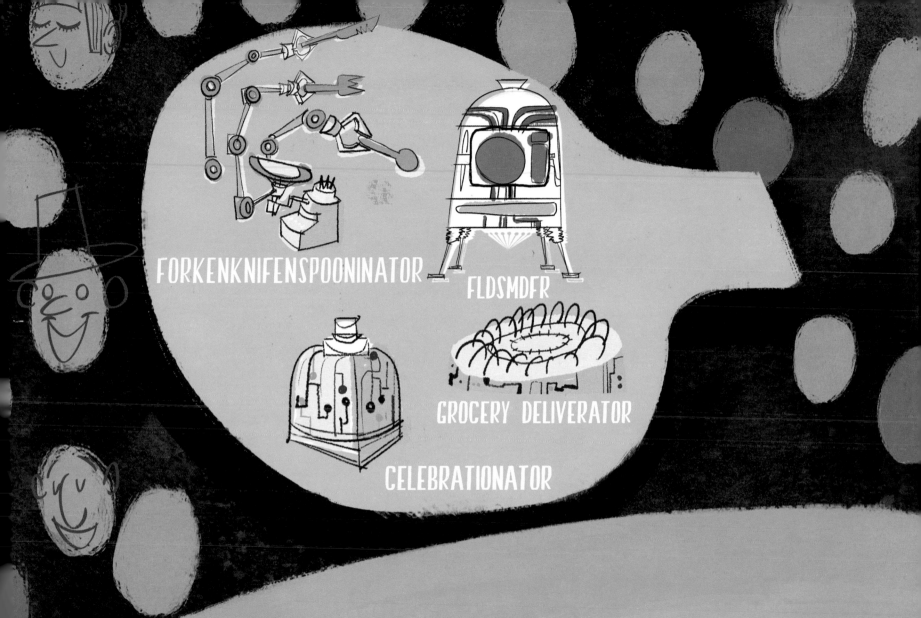

FORKENKNIFENSPOONINATOR

FLDSMDFR

GROCERY DELIVERATOR

CELEBRATIONATOR

Welcome, invention enthusiasts of all ages! We are delighted that you could join us today for a very special celebration honoring the greatest inventor of all time and two-time saver of the world—the one and only Flint Lockwood!

Here is Flint as a child. Wasn't he cute? Even as a little boy growing up in Swallow Falls, Flint had big ideas, like Spray-on Shoes. They were great—no need to tie shoelaces ever again. The only problem was Flint didn't invent a way to take them off!

Another one of Flint's early inventions was for his trusty lab partner, Steve.

Steve is here with us today! Hello, Steve!

Flint invented a Monkey Thought Translator that turned Steve's thoughts into words so people could understand him.

Flint, why don't you turn on the Thought Translator so we can find out what Steve is thinking right now?

HUNGRY! HUNGRY! HUNGRY!

Hmmm . . . does anyone have a banana?

The invention that truly put Flint on the map was the Flint Lockwood Diatonic Super Mutating Dynamic Food Replicator, or the **FLDSMDFR** for short. The amazing **FLDSMDFR** turned water into food, causing cheeseburgers, bacon, and pizza, and even ice cream to rain down from the sky. There was so much delicious food that the mayor changed the name of Swallow Falls to Chewandswallow. Tourists from all over came to visit the town that rained food, and grab a tasty snack as a souvenir!

But when the **FLDSMDFR** began supersizing everything, Flint knew he had to put an end to his machine. Everyone was in a panic. But not Flint! He knew those Spray-on Shoes would come in handy for something! He aimed the spray bottle directly at the **FLDSMDFR**'s spout and sealed it shut. Flint was a hero to everyone in Chewandswallow . . . especially to one lovely weathergirl, Sam Sparks.

Flint's talent as an inventor soon caught the eye of Chester V, the head of Live Corp. Chester was Flint's idol. He had always dreamed of working for Chester as one of his **Thinkquanauts**. Flint thought they had a lot in common, especially when he discovered that they had both invented the same **Wedgie-Proof Underwear**!

Flint was thrilled to finally be meeting Chester in person . . . until he realized he was meeting a hologram. Chester explained that since he was always so busy, he invented HOLOGRAMS so he could be in more than one place at a time.

Chester knew great talent when he saw it! Soon Flint was working at Live Corp, creating new inventions around the clock, such as the **Invisible Coffee Table** (which, um, still has a few kinks that need to be worked out). The best thing about the **Invisible Coffee Table**? It's invisible!

The worst thing about the Invisible Coffee Table **? It's invisible!**

Flint was determined to be the next Thinkquanaut. He worked long hours every day, and submitted new inventions every night.

"Can your ideas change the world?" asked the Chester V motivational poster at Live Corp headquarters.

"Yes, Chester V poster, they can!" answered Flint.

MOTIVATION POD

Another one of Flint's inventions at Live Corp was the Re-freeze-a-fan, which promised to make ice cubes a thing of the past. Another splendid idea, except this one worked–dare I say it–a little too well!

Keep trying on this one, Flint. We think it's really . . . uh . . . cool!

Flint always tries to come up with inventions that make people's lives happier and easier. Don't you hate lugging heavy groceries back home from the store? Flint invented the Grocery Deliverator! What a concept!

Of course, this one needs a few tweaks too. We want our groceries delivered, Flint. We don't want them to catch us by surprise!

And once we have our groceries, what do we want to do? Why eat them, of course! Which is why Flint came up with the Forkenknifenspooninator. Not only does it come in handy at dinnertime, a giant one is the perfect tool for heavy lifting!

Ah, this next invention is Steve's favorite. The Celebrationator! A party in a box for any occasion. Just push the button and suddenly you and your friends will be covered with streamers, glitter, and confetti. No . . . wait! Don't push the button yet, Steve!

So what truly makes Flint the greatest inventor of all time? It isn't the number of inventions he's created. (Although you can see he's created many!) It's the fact that Flint never gave up on his number one dream . . . to make the world a better place. Even though some of his inventions didn't work at first, that only made him more determined to do better the next time. And that's something we can all learn from Flint—believe in yourself and never give up.

SPARKS ♡ WOOD

STEVE ∆ ME

FLINT @ WORK

Three cheers for **Flint Lockwood**, the greatest inventor of all time! It's time to **celebrate**, Steve!